A Snowman named just Bob

Written by
Mark Kimball Moulton

Illustrated by
Karen Hillard Crouch

Lang Books
Delafield, Wisconsin
A Lang Company

Text by Mark Kimball Moulton
Illustrations by Karen Hillard Crouch
©Copyright 1999
All Rights Reserved
Made in the U.S.A.

Published by Lang Books
A Division of R.A. Lang Card Company, Ltd.
514 Wells St.
Delafield, WI 53018
1-800-967-3399

www.lang.com

ISBN: 0-7412-0283-2

Second Edition

10 9 8 7 6 5 4 3 2 1

*Any similarity to a friend or relative named "Bob" is purely coincidental and absolutely delightful!

Gladly presented to:

On this day:

from:

It was late
that one Thanksgiving,
when Bob first
came to me...
a joyful day
of food and fun,
with friends and
family.

We had feasted well, as I recall,
on Mother's fine cooked fare, then settled down to rest
awhile and nap without a care. No one knew what was
to be as daylight grew quite dim. That soon our lives would
change so much... simply because of him.

The weatherman reported no snow was due that night, but as we slept, the clouds rolled in, obscuring all the light. And though the weatherman had tried, he never could have said just what was forming in the sky, directly overhead!

The Moon grew bright,
then disappeared,
then broke into a laugh.
The stars began to dance a jig,
the clouds just split in half.

In retrospect, I do believe
that magic came that night.
No ordinary storm, you see,
could stir up such a sight.

The sky began to whip around,
then settled on its way.
The wind skipped lightly through the trees,
inviting me to play.

It took a while,
    but late that eve,
        a tiny snowflake fell...

It may sound odd,

but this is true...

you could almost feel the smell...

There was freshness in the country air
on that November night,

As one flake turned to many...

and spread a cloak of white.

Just when it seemed
the storm might pass,
or at least be mild,
the Moon came out and
gave a wink,
then stood back and smiled.
And this is when I dare to say
that Bob first came to be,
as peace fell lightly like a
robe over every hill and tree.
He fell upon my windowsill,
he landed in my hair,
he frosted all my
neighbors' homes,
and blew throughout
the air.

And after all the mystery,
I hoped that I would view
a friendly face among those flakes,
providing me a clue.

The snow took on an eerie cast,
first pink, then blue, then gold.
Then anxious little whirlwinds
Leaped around my feet so bold!

'Twas then I heard a whisper,
So gentle, soft and kind...
he wanted me to help him,
of course, I wouldn't mind...

To gather up those many flakes
and roll them in a ball,
'till he could be, and be with me,
in shape and form and all.

"But, Bob!" I cried, "I just don't know where you are in all of this!
'Cause all of you is everywhere throughout this snowy-ness!
You're scattered over everything... so how do I begin,
to gather all your goodness and make a perfect friend?"

Suddenly the whispers stopped.
Sir Moon then took a bow.
He bestowed on me this message
I offer to you now...

I ran into my mother's house to wake
those sleepy folk, and bid
them come and help me to
roll and pat and poke.
And build that grand
ol' snowman and do
a right good job.
To bring to life
my special friend,
my snowman named
just "Bob."

We laughed and sang
and ran about
as Bob began to be.
We gathered up
what we would need,
everything was free!

Some coal for eyes,
a carrot nose,
some sticks,
a scarf,
a hat.
A smile so wide
it warmed your heart,
a coat,
and that was that.

Perhaps you think so far that magic ruled the day,
so far will seem like 'nothing' to what was on its way!

For this is when our new friend, Bob, decided to awake...
he opened up his twinkling eyes,

his belly, it did shake.

His voice I do remember
was something of a dream.
His countenance, so pleasing,
unearthly it did seem.

And though you might be doubtful,
a talking friend made out of snow?
This is what we heard from Bob,...
he wanted us to know...

"You've given me my eyes
so I might see and blink.
A mouth, a hat, a carrot nose,
so I might speak and think.

The scarf indeed is cozy,
it's sure to keep me warm.
And thank you all for giving
me such a shapely form.

I hope it snows a'plenty
so I might stay and share,
in all your loving friendship,
your thoughtful, tender care.

But when it warms, or if in spring,
you miss that I'm not near...
put a sign in your front yard
that reads just "Bob was here.""

Well, that was it...
'twas all Bob said
that dreamy,
starry
night.

He'd said his piece, he closed his eyes,
yet everything seemed right.

We all joined in Celebration for his message was quite clear, that just like all good faithful friends... Bob is always near.

BOB was here.

forget me not